The True

World:

A Scientific

&

Philosophical Wonder

Mohammed Hossain

Second Printing:

February 2020

Contents:

<u>Chapter One:</u>

This World and the Creations of Fire

Fire is the cause and reasons of this creation. This whole creation has two realities, one that is created from decomposition of fire and the other without the absence of it. The exact time frame of the creations of fire remains unknown until we have access to the information's stored in different matter or matters. To have that access to the universal creation is the common pursuit of every human unless someone more intelligent than us declares wisdom over us. Fire is the taste and education of all living creations. We humans have the best sensation, yet it remained an elusive theory in creation. Because of the controllability of the events that are of no one's reached. And the creation will remain in doubt of the perception that we present. But it's true it can be controlled, only for him who has the power and knowledge to withhold creation, where we all find our purpose in living.

Any super creation that has won the death by any means or by all means can evolve into the infinite reality and can find the cure for death and its causes. We can research from what nature and matters functions are and why they should destroy some and help others. In doing that we find the true purpose of this creation and its lessons that admire us by saving one from another or from the catastrophes by nature. We may not find all the answers of our concerns until one intelligent theory in creation gives reasonable explanation of life and its purpose. We all like to dream and it's the simplicity in our thought. A life must not lose the motion. Good and bad are the true philosophies of life and we find hope while watching the motions that help us in growth. The solutions to life can be simple or complicated. When we have hope it is simple and if not, our intelligence comes into a challenge in safety from the acts that are of inhuman in nature.

We live not because we have to but because we feel the pleasure and zeal in it. A true intelligence can recover us from the power of death and destructions. A safe passage of life needs an understanding be it the nature or solely the matters that are of biological in its function which in turn enriches our memories. None whatsoever would be interested in losing it. When we die, our existence becomes a mystery. Why there is a death? And how to stop it? We often look for answers in a faith. Is faith man made? Or who can claim life and death? In science we understand that death is a motion lost. Can science reverse it? The answer is yes and only possible by him who knows how to reverse his own death. If we ever achieved it, we are an intelligent species. This may be true when we can stop the motion that causes us death. But the issue here is that this entire creation is on that deadly pursuit, notably the nature and the matters. We may have question; how far can we go in saving a life? Up to the point where we find the forces that are responsible for a death. If someone can do it, we all win the limitless existence.

The theory of creation is an intelligent analysis of finding the reality apart from what we feel on earth. It is my prudent belief that the current creation in one hand didn't start from its own. It's a very careful layout of what we see and feel on earth. On the other hand, every creation is being presented by a realtor. The only way to face it is the competition in giving a wise perception of facing that realtor. If it is universally agreed that the realtor is none but one of us facing his own destiny and choice. The time is a barrier between the realtor and the reality. None of us want to see that if the realtor of such magnitude should ever fail. The facts and the events are correctly predicted, and we find such memory in rejuvenation. One may fail but not the reality that we hope for and for every one's rescue, we try even harder to see the fruits of our labour and intelligence provides us with promising growth. And a memory must not be lost. If we recover from that, we have one question, who will be the realtor? The toughest truth is it is in the form of casualties until we find the answers of our questions.

Science is the discipline that maintains the order in creation. It is nothing more than logic. We now have question, who set it in motion? Can he recover us from the decay, death and destructions? The answer won't be too difficult; it is the universal motion in its routine functions. These motions represent superior discipline and an experience must not be lost. The motions set in order may be the most significant momentum in our lives. If we could reach to its core reason, there is one thing truth; it's a most beautiful dream that we are a part in it. Still we will remain doubtful about the future as long as there is no proof of the future that we predict and analyze. The knowledge is power when we understood the complete reality and the proof is just a mere happening. Time wins in every cycle of our thoughts. Time is of no use when we have answer to infinite motion that can last for as long as we need.

This infinite motion can be a passage in our intelligence. We dream it till the time we achieve it into reality. How this creation came into a reality? Why do we die? And what happens next? Even if the creation started from its own, we are happy that it maintains a universal discipline. We learned to predict and protect and save. How will we save and recover from what we have lost? It is a challenge to us all. Even if this creation started from its own there is a clear proof that it maintains the universal discipline and we can invent its functional mechanism by looking at what causes in growth and decay, also hunger, death and destruction. We will be an absolute scientist when we understand the motion that caused us death and the motion that recovers from death. It all lies in motion controlled by time and the time stops when energy that we belong is non-destructive by any motion and the infinite reality in clear perception.

The fire is the main cause and effect of this creation. The entire creation is created by decomposition of fire. How is fire created? There are two phases in creation, one that is experimental and the other being the proof. The proof is the everlasting and the experimental is the time frame existence. In other words, the two phases in creation is, one that is created from fire and the other from light. The current creation is the passage through fire. This fire is again created from light. Therefore, fire alone is not the sole purpose in creation. Fire is the motion that dismantles, and we feel apparent reality to permanent reality. The creation of light is the permanent existence. The fire than created from light to have a passage and given with time. When time expires fire will dissipate from existence and the creations of light will assume its contents and the universal creation in refined momentum will begin.

All the matters and life are given with time frame existence and ever existence. The creations of fire have all the materials that are originally belong to the light elements. In fact, the matter and life created from light are the realities that are in passage through fire. But there are certain lives that are the only reality of being the sole creations of fire. Bad luck to know that those lives which possess life will not exist beyond the perimeter of fire. Because it will be difficult to cause and reason when fire is resolved. In other words, the creations of fire have its reality which lasts as long as fire lasts. They become zero in equation, the reason why it's an impossible to imagine their existence without fire.

Since this whole universe and the world are created from decomposition of fire, they are represented in plants, animals and human's alike. When fire is resolved from creation the creations of fire will also be subsided. Why is such that fire can't stay any longer than its existence? There comes the question of reality. Fire can't stay in the existence of light that is perfected for ever existence. Because fire always has timing whereas light don't.

In science, the current creation is carbonic in principle. Everything that is created from fire is in the carbon bond. Theoretically, carbon maintains the bond between life and matters. All the metals that we see are actually the elements of light that are given with carbon sustenance for the creations of fire. This carbon can be decomposed to nothing and which will result in elimination of any reality that carbon holds. They all will disappear from creation and fire will be extinguished and there will be no fire invented or present in any part of creation.

In humans, plants, and animals of the creations of fire, carbon holds the structure in Gene sequence on the other hand those created from light has non carbon genes or true carbon genes. Because there are two types of carbons, true carbon, and the fake carbon. True carbon is created from light and the fake carbon is created from fire.

Therefore, when carbon is resolved the types holding the fake carbon bond will also be resolved, the creations of the true carbon bond will remain unaffected. This fake carbon creation is only the reality of fire and when fire is resolved they cannot function any longer than the carbon bond holds, and it becomes an unknown mystery until recreation of fire is back in creation again. On the other hand, the creation of light becomes the permanent and everlasting existence. The same way the humans, plants and animals of light embrace infinite growth. Therefore, the two realities are very carefully laid out. We may ask how it is true. It's true in two ways, one, fire is destructive, and second, light helps growth.

Fire is the experimental light which is between dark and light. When the fire is resolved the light takes its place and the new creation begins. This world and the creations of fire are represented by the carbon bond which is the fake carbon. Soon this carbon bond will dissimilate and the whole universe will go through a catastrophic end and the creations of light will be rescued. There will be widespread malfunction of materials including whatever stage they are in solid, liquid or gaseous substances. It will be a difficult trend since there are also lives that belongs to the same carbon bond and that will be the end of existence of anything that is created from fire or decomposition of fire. Why is such? Because this creation will be resolved with the end of fire and its task. The exact timeline will also be discovered before its end, which is in the form of casualties.

What is the necessity of the creations of fire? Philosophically there are two realities, one is apparent and the other is permanent. The permanent reality is the essence of light. The creations of fire are the redundancy of the lost memory, which we regain orderly by the cycles in creation. Creation faces its phases from one form to the other, where the latter involves the success of intelligent creation. The memory of which is ever growth and permanent existence, but the fact is that everything then goes back to the incipient stage and one holds the others victory.

We may not like to see anyone lost in the pursuit of creation and we ask all should have a place in their respective world. The real issue is that none can relive an impossible reality because, fire is the question of power which is only destructive in nature and we can't have a dream always under in challenge of destruction and casualties. Therefore, it is the only reason of mistrust and fire gives the reasons in it. Now we have question, who has the control? The person with most accurate knowledge will have the control. Since it involves the date, time and effect, soon we will be able to discover the certainty of those events that caused us death and peril and find the ways of recovery. A true knowledge will never be lost and that's our hope in the future.

What will happen if fire is resolved from creation? The new creation will then take place that is created from light. Indeed, it will be the refurbished growth that will last for ever or at least till the time we are pleased with creation. The creations of fire will then turn into a mystery. Carbon controls the life and matters of fire and the life created from light controls carbon. So, a true light can never be destroyed

Chapter Two:

The Creations of Light: The True World

There is one purpose in creation: the Truth that is the only way in hope. It's true we existed, and we will be existing again into the infinite growth. The True World is the answer to that fact. The True World is the absolute perfection in our dreams. Since there are two realities in creation, we never could invent the ultimate truth. Yes, it is true in both science and philosophy, the true world in existence. We humans are best in knowledge, intelligence and pursuit. Our quest in truth never rested and will never rest until we discovered the endless possibilities that will open up the real sense in creation.

Light is the only source in creation that embedded us into life and matters. Even the fire and this world is also the product of light on fire. Soon the fire will be resolved, and we will follow through the transition into the life and matters of light. When light regains its momentum, we will watch the display of invention and ambition of many that lamented the world into a perfect glory. We will have absolute nature and non-destructive matter and life without any death or decay. The creation and the passage to the True World will be very smooth one like a sleeping baby who finds himself into that world. It will be only possible for the creations of light to travel and live in that world. As for the creations of fire they will remain in our memory.

The evolution will let us win our death and we will find the True World in perfect order. All the life and matters created from light will embrace infinite growth and there will be no death or destruction. This world is a dismantling education and the True World a perfected glory. Why this world cannot be converted to true world? Because everything that we see and find here is the ultimate creations of fire and this fire has to be resolved. When the fire is on the casual motion it will affect our existence here for the true light, therefore, we seek the safer place that's the True World in complete harmony. The safe passage into that world will be open and we will be joined by family and friends, the true glory in creation that is waiting for its inhabitants, the True World in absolute perfection.

There will be a period of transition from this world to the True World. The True World exists in perfect condition as is the creations of light. All the matter and life of light will then be relocated in that world upon completion of their tasks. Soon death will be stopped for the life of light creation and voyage to the True World will be open. All the creations of light are relocated in the True World upon completion of their tasks. The True World has all predominated science and the modern spaceships that can travel between the worlds and the universes. Our intelligence may fail in the pursuit of adventure but when it will be opened for our inhabitations it will become much simpler.

The True World is the absolute perfection in science, and no one dies, or any destruction can ever take place in that world. We will be joined by family and friends and we will have great joy and happiness that will last into infinity. Before the transition begins everyone will know their specific tasks and we all will be transported in good care. That world is the permanent reality in creation. In fact, we always existed there, and we come to the world of fire only for a lesson of few years and the True World will be complete memory in succession. We may not know what the ultimate truth could be, but our intelligence will never fail in the pursuit of adventure. The True World exists as the creation of light exists. We just lost memory and we always existed there and now are the time to recover our origin.

This creation is the design and effect of many in one goal and one dream that combines us into the family of nations. But it will be a painful confession to imagine this creation is divided into two realities and the families created from fire will have no sign of existence in the near future. When the fire is resolved their existence will also be stopped. Truly bad luck for them if realization ever felt in that way and nothing more than to bid goodbye for the lessons of life. This is the only reason of social and global instability and insecurity. They will never agree of such demise rather create inhumane scenarios wherever their influence takes them up to.

The light creation upon a lesson finds hope and the fire creation develops vengeance the main reason of the impossible reality that if fire ever allowed into that civilised world of light, it will be the end of a true philosophy. In the True World there will be only one civilisation and that will have no questions to ask; who is the realtor? Honour and respect will always represent the perfect glory and day to day tasks. We will have every quality of matter and materials but not fire, because this is the limitations in hope.

The True World is a true discipline that is understood by all and instead of clash of interest we will have respect and honour and that will fit the intelligence of every creation into its perfect order and harmony. Since everything is created from light, every character will maintain its unique role in a befitting manner. There will be no failure of matter or mechanism. They will be complete in energy and won't consume or leave any by-products. The energy that we belong will be complete. The growth will be stabilized and there will be no regeneration. The same family with its members will exercise ever existence and the day to day tasks.

Everyone will understand each other and look for the intelligence that will answer any body's queries and questions in a responsible manner. Each moment will resound its effect on everyone, if any senses are in wrong order? There will be no chances to ask.

This world is the copy version of the true world. Now that the copy should end, and we learn that a true light can never be destroyed. It is the transition in education and the True World is a perfected glory which is an everlasting principle. The True World will be filled with joy and triumph. There will be no accident or casualty either by men or nature. Light will remain into infinite growth and reality. It is also scientifically true that light can sustain any reality into it; it's only the controllability that remained questionable. This is true that when time is favourable this control will appear in a simple understanding and the transition to that reality will be as easy as our knowledge itself.

How the fire is lit? Or how the light is lit? It may define wisdom. The wisdom of knowledge and power. Since it's a huge creation, the answer may be a simple theory. The fire is created from light and the light is the unique motion that keeps every true creation in its growth. The growth that will ensure and let us know about the knowledge of a happening truth. This happening truth is the wisdom. The wisdom of knowledge and power. It will assume his responsibility who knows everything truth time immemorial. Even if this creation just happened it has a smaller cause. The cause to know what would happen next after one another. Even time will become a useless motion where we will live as long as we wanted. That means everyone's happiness will be a perfect reality and we will find creation is everyone's shared interest. That's why we mean by education that infinity is our reach and the motion that caused us death could be reversed into a perfect and everlasting glory. The light that builds hope for all and desert for others to burn into an impossible reality.

Light is the symbol of creation. The True World is the true perfection in our dream where light resurrects into infinite motion. We will have every material perfected into the elements of light that can build a dream which no one could ever imagine. The entire universe will assume its new look upon relieving the fire from its task. The life and matter that is in carbon bond and controlled by carbon will dissimilate from creation. It may surprise us that there are also lives that will be in mystery because their existence is limited as long as the fire existed. When fire is resolved those life will be an end in existence or future growth.

Now, we may have question, what is light? Light is simply vision to see and feel the unlimited. Light is everything in creation and it is the everlasting energy. Every matter and life are the ultimate creation of light. It is both the motion and the existence. The reason why we cannot differentiate light on earth is because it is caused through motion, where fire is given sustenance. This fire is also created from light and will exist in a time measured pursuit. When we measure light, we find it in electrons.

The infinite growth and existence are the ultimate perfection of light. This light alone can design the permanent creation that can last into infinity. We all existed in creation, and when fire created from light, our memories dispersed. Now is the time when we regain our origin in creation, the creation of light which is everlasting existence. Soon the creations of fire will be resolved, and light will regain its dominance. All the matter and life that is the origin of light will form the new reality and the True World will come into existence.

The life and matter lost in the cycle of creation will be recovered. No memory will be a mystery because a light is the everlasting growth that can last into infinity. When fire and its creations are recreated, the life will go through the same reality that we face in today's growth and experience.

The True World is the absolute perfection and it is the dream of whole mankind. Every one's estimation will form it into a reality that can never be destroyed or dismantled by any force or might. It will even beat the race of time. Even the microscopic creation of life and matter will have passion and comfort of ever existence. The creations of light will then decide their interest of recreating the fire and its creations, not until a single question could arise in its concern in recreating the fire and its existence.

The True World exists in our thoughts and intelligence. Since light is caused through motion, it is the creations of fire that limits the light from its definitive role, the reason of our death and destruction. When the fire is resolved the creations of light will occupy its origin in creation. Our memories are the only difference between the creations of light and fire. There will be lives that are affected and will diminish from existence and that are the creations of fire. Every matter, both biological and chemical is the existence of light that are driven through the motions of fire and they will be perfected into the true matters of light upon resolution of fire. We will notice that the lives that resound the fire will not exist into the true creation of light because their reasons will be stopped and cannot exist beyond the creations of fire.

Chapter Three:

The Nature

The Nature is the relationship between the life and matter. The ultimate reality is growth and decay. The nature otherwise is the sensation to feel what could be possible in being the possession of life. The nature that we feel on earth is the evolution of facts and events representing the cycle of growth. The nature also represents superior intelligence. It can stop growth, or it can replenish. Since this creation has two realities, the creations of fire and the creations of light, the current nature teaches us the possibilities of infinite growth; the creations of light. We are actually in transition from time frame existence to permanent existence.

The creations of fire are the time frame existence and the creations of light are the permanent existence and such is the reality in nature. Since we all evolve, our intelligence fails to stop the casualties, because, we have no control or enough information's as how and when the creations of fire and nature complete evolution. Thus, the evolution will stop when light supersedes all the growth and the motion from its existence in fire, the fire will stop and become a useless motion and completely die down from its origin. The creation of light then becomes a reality and a world of our choice without any death or destructions.

The true nature then takes its place in creation and it will last as long as every creation of light and its senses overcomes its interests in living and loving.

The nature of fire teaches us the reactions of scientific elements involving its functions in different forms. The main element that causes major reactions in terms of growth and its parity is the Carbon. Carbon is created from dark matter with the help of light in formation of the nature of fire. This carbon is the main cause and effect of current nature. Carbon helps the fire to sustain. The transformation of matters from Chemical stage to Biological form is the motion of carbon. Carbon also stores memory. This memory is the sole reality of the creations of fire. That's why a memory cannot sustain into reality of any longer than science holds. Science comes in question, why is a memory can't hold infinity? Because memory cannot sustain beyond infinity, the reason is its sensation is limited as the creations of fire is limited. This is the most important reason in death and decay. How could we stop death? When we are complete in energy, we stop death. The complete energy stands the universal reality of creation that cannot be destroyed by any force or by any means. The reason is fire always has the timing because of its consumption and function. If fire is extinguished the light will take over its place and then the light will maintain its growth. Since light is the complete sense, it does not require any other source for energy transformation, and it is the infinite reality.

The nature of fire is the major function of the Carbon cells. This carbon cells holds bonds between every creation of fire, including human's, plants and animals. In this creation, there are two forms of life, one that is in fake carbon bond and the other without the carbon bond or in true carbon bond. The life in fake carbon bonds will live as long as carbon bond is functional, that is as long as fire exists. When fire is extinguished, the life created in carbon bond will be resolved and nothing of fire will have the possibility to exist. Then light will refurbish its growth in humans, plants and animals and the new reality in creation will take place that can last into infinity and non-destructive by any force. Why? Because, a light doesn't cause any motion to sustain and it can last into infinity without consuming or leaving any by-products and it's the complete energy, which is the major concern in any creation, notably the creations of fire. Also, light controls time and time controls fire.

The nature of fire exclusively in plants is in different in function. The plants grow through carbon bonds. The carbon in plants do not construct into the other elements like Hydrogen or Oxygen but helps those bonds through the formation that means if carbon is extracted from those plants, the plants still will survive but the growth will stop, that means carbon helps but doesn't construct into it, also they are in true carbon bond mostly in the gene structure. In some humans and animals this carbon bond is permanently constructed, and they cannot be filtered or eliminated as it would result in destruction and that are the sole creations of fire and can't exist beyond the creations of fire. On the other hand, there are a majority of humans and animals that are not constructed by these types of carbon bonds but controls carbon into the biological system in growth. If carbon is filtered from them, they will not be destroyed rather would be difficult to live until given with the matters that are perfected from fire by eliminating the fake carbons from them. So, it would be possible to live and the true carbon then replenishes its creation by the carbons of the creations of light.

Here on earth we face hunger that helps growth. All the living creations are fed by nature and the nature processes the elements through plants and animals. If hunger is stopped it will be a difficult trend since we are not perfected into complete energy that doesn't require any source to live or energy transformation. This remained an unregulated momentum of life. In the True World this energy will be in a fixed growth. That means we will be complete energy which will not require any other source for consumption or rejection of energy and energy will never be wasted or lost. This will be the permanent and fixed growth that will not require any other source for gaining momentum, but we will enjoy food to feel the pleasure and that food will be completely digested without leaving any by-products.

The nature in the True World will be processed in machines and we will not require any plants or animals for the ingredients. The mechanisms that deliver those ingredients will run indefinitely and they will process the nature as per our choice in quality and taste. When we consume those foods they will be digested and our physical activity will disperse the matters into the atmosphere in gases and the nature will redirect them back into the system and we will not need any toilets or washrooms for such rejection of substances in our physiology. It will be a permanent and fixed growth that won't require any other source like plants or animals. Growth will be stabilized and there will be no deaths or diseases, but we will share intelligence.

Since we find all living creations divided by two realities one that is created from fire and the other from light. Carbon controls the creations of fire and the creations of light controls carbon. This carbon also holds memory and this memory controls every creations of fire towards a pursuit whatever memory can lead into notably the time given sustenance not to mention any chance into infinity. It's only the creations of light that controls carbon rather controls the memory into infinite growth. This carbon doesn't only cause growth but all the diseases and aging in all creations of fire and a formidable casualty in true creations. Although none can stop the death of any, death of true creation is just a casualty in timely pursuit which they actually did not die but transferred to a safe haven, the True World in existence.

All the calamities are the symbolic equation to life, and it will be stopped when death of true creations is stopped. The true nature will be a reality in our everyday dream of seeing and enjoying the ever life and its parity into infinity. The True World has all the adventures in realism. That means any of our estimations will not be left untouched. We will find every form and representation in our imaginations into a reality. We will enjoy ever life and ever growth as long as our ambitions desire and hope.

There will be no soil, dust or mud and the ground will be totally carpeted and no open grounds ever visible. The grassy fields will soothe the animals and plants. The flowering plants will be nicely decorated. There will be parks and gardens with permanent and stable flowers and fruits. We will not pluck off flowers or fruits, they will be in a victoriously displayed till infinity. Since nature will be processed in our homes and markets and we will get the pleasures from them without disharmonising any plants or animals. The machines will process nature in absolute terms, and they will never finish. If you require a glass of wine, it will be an easy dispenses both the glass and the wine. Put the glass or the broken pieces of glass into the machine the machine will recycle in an instant basis.

The True World nature will be an absolute perfection and there will be no death, disease or destruction in any form or by any causes. The carbon cells will not have any major role since there will be no fire present in any form or reality, it will be the sole function of light and its matters.

There will be no heat, rain or thunder and the electrical effects will be the biological growth. Water will reach the plants and materials in an electronic motion that will be in superior sense and relief. We will not face hunger but wisdom growth that will not cause us aging. The same family and its members will exercise the ever existence into infinity. The True World nature will be an absolute perfection of every one's choice in dream and reality. The trees will be without any carbon in it and it will remain as in its shape and size without any change and damages to it by any means or ways. Your water fountains will never run out of water or juices no matter how much the consumptions are, it will be forever filled beyond any one's necessity or needs. There will be no waste and everything will be completely recycled. It will help us through the passage of matter, material and wisdom both in Biology and Chemistry. And that's the function of complete nature.

Chapter Four:

The Gravity and Motion

The most amazing part of the creation is the gravity and motion, and this is the main reason of circumference between the reality and the impossible fact. The space remained an impossible venue till this modern day of science in the pursuit of creation. Because of gravity we are restricted in free fall and we dismantle in a sudden impact on the ground and around any highest climb. The rate of fall damages our survival even from a few feet above the ground. That's why we remain victim of casual fall. Also, the atmospheric pressure limits our ability to go beyond the distances into the space and even a return of an object is an impossible fact.

The creations of fire are simply the dismantling reality and the pressure that we feel around us limits our ability to explore beyond the perimeter of our existence. But it's true that the space unlimited will soon open up our ambition to go and reach where no human could ever go before. The dream of the True World is the reality in our thoughts and actions. Here in this world the motion is casual, and every move has its own resolution. The creations of fire are time frame existence and that's the reason we cannot do anything to prevent a mishap or occurrence that leads to death or destruction.

The True World has a central control station from where all the creations from its beginning is being recorded and controlled by time given measure and that's the reason why we fail to invent the reality. But soon time will finish its task relieving the fire from its role and the creations of fire thus will end and the creations of light will take over the control of time and there will be no events except peace and happiness. All the creations of light then will be revealed into a permanent growth and existence. The True World will then start functioning without any death, destruction or casualties.

When all the fires are gone including the humans and animals created from fire, the True World will begin its function in complete harmony. The true world is composed of all the matter and materials that we see and feel on earth except the matters that compose fire, and they will stop decaying or decomposing by any motion. The True World will evolve like a normal planet and the whole universe will form the new reality where time will be a useless motion.

In the True World both the biological aspects and the technical motions will represent superiority in performance and productivity. The world will be designed by grid references; even a minor element will be easily identifiable including any microscopic creations. Any place or any matters will be easily traceable and identifiable according to their locations and position; they will maintain their functions from their respective places universally. All living and matter will be easily found in their respective places and will function according to the purpose given to them. If one drank a cup of tea and the elements get out of our system, they will go back to from where they originated. Everything will have a grid reference from where they function and a suitable return upon completion of their assigned role will be back to their origin. The whole world and the whole creation will move according to the grid reference, where they existed to be specific of a location and place, including the matter, materials and life. So, no one will be lost from their origin in existence.

There will be all modes of communication and transportation which will move according to grid references and a simple programming input will direct the motion to that specific location and it will be so accurate that its performance and reliability will be absolutely to the point without even a fraction of displacements or errors. There will be no freight movements because it will have no use at all. There will be airplanes and spaceships that are one hundred percent accurate without any doubt or concern in its function. Since everything will be complete in energy, they will not require any other power source for energy transformation and the universal motion will be infinity.

The road, air and space traffic will be electronically controlled; moreover, they will be self-controlled with just input from its origin and destination. There will be no traffic signals at the intersections since each traffic will pass and maintain an automatic separation from each other. The aircrafts will not require wings for a float because it will take off and land according to the controlled ascend and descent by the True World central control grid. Even the missions to the space and into the universe will just be a programming event that will initiate and redirect to its origin and destination.

The trains and buses will also maintain similar traffic clearance from each other. The motion will be absolutely accurate and the performances to the point. There will be no free fall since everything is a controlled ascend and descent. If one tries a jump from high altitudes, there will be no need for a parachute, and it will be absolutely controlled fall. How our walking standards affected? None, nothing. The gravity will let us always close to the grounds but not impact in such a manner that could lead us to disembark or frail. Because our grid-controlled world and space has pinpoint accuracy and it's a controlled gravity and motion by every count and rate, therefore, it maintains an accurate balance and force.

In the true world there is nothing called absolute vacuum, and everything will maintain a nominal pressure that won't require pressurisation for any travel into or out of the world and the universe. Similarly, the atmospheric pressure will also maintain a balance between our physical condition and movement from one place to another by ascend to any altitude, therefore, the motion will also maintain equilibrium between our body, the space travelled and the outside pressure. If we stop breathing in distance of space where there is no oxygen present, our breathing will stop and we will talk through electromagnetic waves and that won't hurt the biological system and it will maintain same quality and approach while we communicate between one another. All the limits that are set on this world and the creations of fire will be overcome. Death will be an impossible fact and the motion will travel in space in the speed of light or as per our choice to manoeuvre into infinity and we will set the limit of space travel.

The pressure on earth and absolute vacuum is the cause and effect of the creations of fire, and the reasons in this creation is the absolute vacuum which sets the limit of motions, and the limit in travel. Even if the limit is found it would be impossible to travel that distance. It's only be possible for the creations of light which can cross any boundary of the universe and return won't need any more than a simple wish.

Chapter Five:

The Space Travel

In the True World we will overcome hunger and death. There will be plenty of time to explore the true creation, the creations of light. There will be ambitions to see and feel the infinite growth and the mysteries of existence. To safeguard our values, we will always be innovative in adventure of the new worlds or new realities. Since we understand and feel the light, if there is another existence beyond our universes, which should and must represent superior aspects than what we see and feel in this creation. If there is a new creation exists beyond the boundary of our universe that should and must show a different theory in creation, if they need light it can't be any different than ours since we are already unique in the creations of light. So, there can't be any better creation than of ours.

But we will always invade the doubts of such mystery by travelling even beyond the speed of light. Our spaceships will fly and follow through universal grids to the distant planets and galaxies. We will find that light can hold any value that is permanent and everlasting. There will be worlds that are plausible and inheritable. We will have resources that can fit in any amount any number of dependents in it and it will never end.

Most memorable will be the travel beyond the existence of light. Some explorers will take even few years in a spaceship to explore into the dark. When nothing is visible upon billions of miles and years of travel, they would feel that it's an infinite distance but won't end if travelled for timeless age, we will ask them for a return, and they would return unharmed and intact. If they wish to invent different glory, they will be given with creative power and will say that the creations of light are infinite and won't end even if they controlled time and growth.

Since death and destruction will not have any chance under any circumstances, our invention will surround every day's task. There will remain ideas that will fill every true creation and its passage throughout the existence of the true world. We will find something new every day and share with everyone. The space will open up its boundaries for everyone and all will have a dream in reality and will be given with a chance to explore if there are any impossible glories there to win and if there is one, we will win it by any virtue.

If ever our spaceships are lost in the dark since they are complete in energy it will logically be impossible to happen such but a moments fear will be overcome as the spaceship has the record of travel into infinity or into the dark and its automatic response will redirect its motion and comeback to the true world. The most important aspect would be the factors in control of the true world. The true world will function in a routine manner and it will never be dismantled until the tiniest possible creation or the huge one's aren't satisfied of their wish and will to live as long as they wanted, and until a single mind doesn't wish to comeback to this world, the creations of fire won't be created that fast.

The spaceships will be the most modern and advanced that no human or any other superior creation could ever design and produce such mechanisms. Most importantly it will have infinite survival in both technology and wisdom. It will have a design that can have anything on board including beds, bars and lounges and it can travel for years or centuries without losing any of the amenities on board. In fact, it will feed itself through electronic transfer of elements and products from the true world, if it ever needed, because, they themselves are complete in productivity and growth and will not require any other source for consumption or rejection. It simply is a complete planet in motion.

We will enjoy space travel in both simulation and in reality. The space will open up its vast existence and domain by allowing every creation of light to enhance their imagination and will. We will discover the limitless boundaries and all the mysteries will be resolved. If we want to land in another planet, the spaceship will locate the quadrants of that planet and will execute a grid-controlled descent and a perfect touch down. If there is no oxygen present in that planet, it won't harm anyone since we can still talk and communicate in electromagnetic waves and we will only breathe if there is air present. Since whole creation maintains a nominal pressure and the absolute vacuum will be absent, the creations of light remain an everlasting perfection. The universal gravity itself will be a controlled factor and everything will be in a controlled reality and the true world or any other planets will not let anything into it in impacts rather a superior force in a balanced motion. Therefore, a sky jump, an exit into the space or a minor jump from a skyscraper will not have any uncontrolled impact upon touch down rather it's a very safe landing. The true world gravity will maintain the control of the free fall and it won't cause any sudden impact upon reaching the ground from any altitude or height. Therefore, no death or injury will occur under any circumstances.

Chapter Six:

The Countries and Cities

The True World will be represented by every country and every city. The True World will be bigger than the current world of fire since it has a place for all true creations ever since the inception in creation. Since light cannot be destroyed by any means or by any force, the death of true creation is just a mere transition from one reality to the other. The true world is the most beautiful in creation. Every country, every city and every civilisation will have their place in that world including the plants and the animals.

Each country will be rich in culture and heritage. They will represent unique tradition in lifestyle. Since there will be no casualties either by nature or by human, the glory will be everlasting. All intelligence will be superb. The leadership will display honour and respect. Interstate and intercontinental visits will be monitored by leadership. The parks and gardens will be filled with surprises and everyone will be astonished of the growth that will display the natures wonder. We will find always something new.

All the cities will bear its appearance in marvelous harmony. All the streets and homes will be lighted in beautiful decorations. The electricity will be produced without any loss of any motion or materials and it will have infinite sustenance without consuming or leaving any by-products. They will not require any cable and there will be no electrical shock even if we touch in bare hands or contacts. The electricity that we have here on earth is caused through motion by the creation of fire and that's why it is unsafe and needs precautionary measures.

We will have all kinds of transportation that can travel infinitely without requiring any other energy source and they will be complete in performance and utility. There will be no freight movements since we won't need them for any reason. Each country will have its fleet of airplanes and spaceships. There will be no helicopters, because, the aircrafts both small and big won't require air to support its flight. The true world will be calibrated from its essence into controlled grids and also programmed for everything that happens or will need directions, the air crafts taking off will be dispersed from one location to another by gravity controlled ascent or descent from one grid to another, only a simple programming is all that we need.

Countries also will display the diverse natural beauties and the cities will be decorated by famous arts and murals. Each night will be a new event and the events will never end. Everyone will be a performer and there will be contests that will show the merit and intelligence by many who dreamt of being one. The cities that are culturally diverse will share the joy of being together even if one from distant neighbourhood. The children will be so intelligent that their expertise will lead them into self-proclaimed monarchies, and they will surprise us by their wisdom by becoming one they hope in their dreams, a king, a queen, and a lord. The dramas will bear the signs of their legacy into human history.

The countries and cities will be fairly decorated and there will never be any open ground found, even no dust or debris will harm us any way. Our clothes and shoes will never get dirty neither we will require any need for washing or bathing. The motion will be absolutely pleasant. Nothing will get dirty or bodies will not require baths to clean up. The cities will be the dwelling places for all, and we will have a place to rest wherever or whatever distance we travel. There will be high rises from where we will enjoy the nightly display of lights and its decorations all around the city.

The light will never turn off unless its day light hour. The space will open up its vastness into the dark sky. The stars will invite us for a visit and the poets, and the philosophers will find answers of their quests in reality. Each city will be a unique symbol of glory. They will be as per the choice of its occupants designed and decorated for anyone's surprises. The cities will have all its amenities close at hand. They will be a great hope in invention.

All the cities in a country will have good governance and ruling. An intelligence can never be defeated, or their will be no cause of such effect. They will be most authentic in nature, never letting anyone down from any post or occupation. The countries will organise great events to mark its importance in their history. The life that was lost in abuse here on earth will find its significance in creation of the true world.

Each home in each city will have its entertainment and communication systems that will keep all in high spirit. The live shows by famous artists will be carefully planned and organised. The home entertainment systems will have records of individual nations or societies that were the past happening on earth will be available on video display. None of the events that took place on earth will be unknown by anyone wishing to listen and view. The countries and cities of historical importance will maintain their motions on record as well as they will be living that are of current in nature. Everybody will be well informed and well entertained of the events of all times. Since we will have beautiful civilisations all around us in the true world, we will have no causes or concern of any kind and there will be no happenings of any nature and it will be a wonderful creation filled in pleasure and comfort. The country will honour all and the cities will reflect its vision inspired by its greatness. Each city and each country will be an extra ordinary invention of many, and it will never end.

Chapter Seven:

Transition from this World to the True World

The True World exists in our memory and dreams which will unfold as per everyone's desire and hope. It is the truth that a true memory can never be lost under any circumstances. The true world is our hope in perfection. The science is the evolution and revolution of matter and life. Our intelligence proves that with each days and moments pass by we come to the next reality, the reality to find death being stopped. If death is stopped it will require that the motion that causes us death must also be stopped. How is it possible? That's simple, the light the permanent source in creation has taken its reality and the true world has started to evolve, that mean, the light has taken over the growth into an infinite reality. This will start with an intelligent creation perfected into the elements of light, with the pronounce of the first incident and that already happened or will be effective within the time frame of the current existence.

When we have a clear proof that death is won, it will start to form into all living creation that the light has started its essence in creation in full harmony. The life that won the death will find the casualties that are of essential task for all to recover from the death and its parity. It will then start to form and invent the causes of death and find its reasons. When the reasons are found, that will show us the clear damage to encounter and brave it in lessons. With the knowledge and the growth, all the deaths will be stopped except the creations of fire. The life that is created from fire will then be resolved, because, when light takes over the energy and growth, the reasons in fire become motionless. Notably, turning out into the mystery of the creations of fire.

The light then starts to form its new beginning with the safe passage of all matters and life that are the creations of light. The True World then gradually starts to form its reality. It will not be a mere happening but eventful of surprises. The fire before disappearing will turn into an unsafe condition which will require a safe passage for the lives that are created from light. A safe world will then be emerged which will be a necessity until the fire has turned off from its existence.

All the creations of light will then enter into the knowledge and information of do's and don'ts around them until light is fully relieved and forms the True World into a perfect harmony. The true world exists in the memory of all true creation that are created from light and their memory and perception will be programming function for evolution of the true world and its amenities to support life and conquer mechanisms of motion and growth.

When all the fires and the creations of fire are resolved, the light then will find its permanent growth which ultimately is the pursuit of all true creations. In the true world we will have access to all the information's from the beginning of creation. In fact, the entire creation in both from fire and light is the design and effect of all true creations. It is never a singular momentum since everyone accounts for the motion and growth, and it's a shared joy into doomsday until the most intelligent recovers from the damage of death and destructions. That's why we have safety laws to bind all into a perfect creation. And those laws are designed from centuries of creations. The one set by our predecessors still hold right because they will recover into the civility of ever existence, only the time was the killer and the time will be their savior again. And they will find their place most truthfully in the true world, because, a true memory never dies, it just changes from one stage to the other. The creations of light can never be destroyed since the light can never be destroyed by any power either, and it is the infinite growth, the virtue in light, the most superior creation in any or all circumstances. The light can never be destroyed and will last into the infinity. If light is destroyed it will be an absurd reality and the truth will never win which is never possible to imagine and totally unreal to believe in that if it ever happens it must be a power that has no vision.

Before the transition begins everyone will be educated and informed of the beginning of new creation. At the same time death will also be stopped. The last child born will be taken care of in a very safe way until he or she finds the wisdom in growth and harmony. The power of mystery will start to take shape and we all will understand the reasons in creation and its follow up through generations. Instead of aging we earn renewed confidence and firm belief that the motions that are of casual in nature will begin its reality into the ever existence. The force of destruction will cease as soon as the fire has been resolved. Everyone will know the events that take place before the transition into the infinite growth begins.

After the successful transition, we all find the true world in perfect harmony and the new beginning will unfold its pursuit in creation. Everything that is created from fire including the humans and the animals will then be resolved into a memory.

Chapter Eight:

The Living Standards

The living standards in the True World will be an astonishing achievement. We will have all qualities of matters in our use. We will live there as long as we want to live, because, the reasons won't stop until there remains a single question in our minds which will be sensed by the matter and the consecutive timings in effect. We will have superior quality of living. Since there will be no death and destruction, we will have great joy, and everyone will enjoy the infinite growth and limitless scientific wonder in discovery and exploration. Every day and every night will bring new realities into our thoughts and imagination.

The homes and the cities will have all amenities. There will be all kinds of entertainments. Our homes will have the machines that will process nature for its ingredients to prepare meals. It will not be left behind anything we want to taste for our pleasure. The qualities will beat anything that we enjoyed on earth. The machines will instantly recycle anything that we don't need. The processing of food and materials will be universally controlled and connected to each house which will never finish. Since we will be infinite in both energy and growth, we will not face aging. The same family and its members will enjoy everlasting life with no end, and none will be sorry for anything.

The gardens by the house will have flowers that will be forever live, and they won't require any water or care. We will have pets that will have superior sense and always play and accompany us. Our cars, phones and the televisions will function without losing any charging or power even there are no electrical connection to them, because, the product of light doesn't need any energy for its use and will be infinite in function.

We will have every quality of matter but not fire because fire is the limit. We will enjoy all the qualities of creation which we enjoyed in this earth before and that will be far more superior in both quality and taste. We will never lose memory or experience. There will be beautiful bond between family, friends and relatives. Each day will pass by in defence of splendor and promise and nothing will be a question by anyone.

Nobody's estimation will be left untouched. There will be events that never took place in any creation which will surprise us as a new creation. We will rest and sleep whenever we feel for it. Most importantly we will not require work to support ourselves, but we will be the freelance and the enthusiasts in every sphere of life. The beauty and the naughty will both find their place in true harmony in our beautifully crafted civilisation that will never be in question by anyone. Also, there will be plenty of high-rise towers that will be an occasional and permanent dwelling for many. Every evening will be a common night for all where we will share the music and fragrances. The beautiful and the ugly both will share their experiences among all in a most peaceful and in befitting social orders. They all will represent the necessity of being a unique example in creation. The true world will never hurt anyone of their essence, and all will possess unique qualities of life.

Since there will be no casualties either by nature or by human, we will enjoy the everlasting growth and decay and destruction will be an impossible thought. The children will be in an age which makes them independent of any care or concern. There will not be any elderly either. The life will start to function to its fullest length and parity and there will be no shortage of anything of our interest. The science will come down to our simple wish and use. No one will be unhappy of any desire and it will be a perfect civilisation that will carry a balance in every respect.

We will live as per our choice and find the things which were impossible before. The true world will be knitted so well that it will never cause us any discomfort and the entire world will be covered by plasters and grasses and there will be no open grounds. Every home will have flower garden and flowers bloom round the year and round the clock. There will be only one season, the ever-beautiful spring and there will be only one motion, the infinite glory. The sky will be so vast that we will travel the limitless by spaceships that can support to travel any distance of our choice.

We will enjoy each day and each moment in true company and friendship of every one of our choice. There will be none so rich or none so poor; we won't feel its necessity since everyone's wish will be filled in with abundance. It is the intelligence layout of the wiser that an equal harmony is in our essence to promote. Of course, the most intelligent will be honoured by all but it won't mean someone is less intelligent, because everyone will have equal share of the true world amenities. The most beautiful will bond between all in a very presentable manner and one won't feel anything absent from their hearts and minds.

The living standards will be highly innovative, and we will find something new every day. Those who have been casualties of this world of fire will be the true ornaments as living angels in the true world. Every night will signify its importance in the true world. The true world is our gallant choice in creation. Every form of life will find its specific place of dominance and it will never miss what a life is meant for it in its existence. Both the matter and life will form its resilient bond and one won't cause the other to sensation rather than a combined choice of ours which will constitute a universal growth that will last as long as we wanted. The forces of the nature will maintain a unique role in both productivity and growth. We will share our experiences with every one of our family and friends. The living and leading life to its fullest will be our everyday credentials filled with surprises and discoveries beyond our own boundaries and it will be an honoured and respectful venture of all of us together. Everyone will find their palaces filled with diamonds and flowers. Nothing will remain a question or no questions will remain unanswered. The true living in what we feel right.

Chapter Nine:

The Ever Youth

The True World will be famous for its youthful nature. It will last for ever. The entire nature will be youthful. Without youth life remains incomplete. Truly this youth is the number one cause and inspiration of life. Here in this world we get it for only few years whereas it will remain pure and permanent in the true world. Also, this youth divides us between good and bad. Productivity was given with youth but when it will be a fixed growth in the true world, we will enjoy it to the fullest. There will be no regeneration and we will enjoy youth as the virtue and meaning of life.

Since there will be no hunger in the true world our only reality will be to enjoy every moment in a most meaningful way. That means we will have ever youth and that will maintain its purity by not requiring any opposite genders touch to feel it and the gender difference will be maintained and it won't require functioning in its touch to feel the pleasure nor it will have any necessity in existence. The genders will simply be symbolic in its nature. A youthful nature is everyone's dream. That nature is the absolute perfection and we will not miss any of the pleasures that we enjoyed on this earth.

Anything that we eat and drink will give us the pleasure and excitement instead of involving into an honourless act without any reason in it. Even the children will have the taste of the true nature that will generate our feelings like a never-ending process. All children will have the taste of youth as per their intelligence in growth and they also will be the great performers. There will be none without the youthful nature. Even the plants and the animals will feel the youthful nature. We will have alcohols and wines that won't let us lose us sense but an indefinite pleasure, an understanding beyond comprehension. We will have that reality and will not let us into indecent acts.

The youthful nature in the true world is best perfection in evil and there will be no questions to ask. The youth of the world of fire is a dishonour and disrespectful in many ways which we feel in both acts and crimes. Those questions will never arise in the true world as the experience in youth will not require the participation of the other gender to feel it right. The reality will be even better than what we feel on earth.

But we will enjoy the great performances of the artists who always wanted to be one. Nobody will lose youth and grow old since it will be fixed growth for ever. The youthful nature will fill our life with so much amusements and excitements that we will feel it like a never-ending process. Everyone will find their loved one's which they dreamt about and find the truth in their company. Even children will have their mock marriages and play partners. The days will be so eventful that it will be hard to miss even one day excitements. By the by none will be too young or too old. The perfect happiness when one enjoyed the life the most here on earth will even beat it by all counts. The youthful nature in the true world will remain infinity and that's the nature we all the creations of light in which it belongs to.

We will enjoy the lessons of any failed love in a dramatic sequence. We will listen to their stories and we will share their joy surrounding the facts. The beauty that was hurt on this earth will find its perfect place and their partner alike. We all will express our gratitude towards the fruitful end, and we will listen to their admiration and accomplishment in a most glamorous way that an experience never missed by anyone, the joy of life and its growth into infinity. There will be no elderly or handicaps. Those who had these experiences on earth will be the most meaningful existence in creation and they won't say that they have missed anything rather found everything back together including love and harmony. They will be the motion and zeal of the true world.

Those brave people who sacrificed everything they had for others benefit will find the true world a place in hope and admiration. They will display their merit and skills in various social and communal events. The mark of youth in them will be the greed of many and their beautiful partners will be together for ever and the bond will never be broken under any circumstances. Everyone will have their own company, sometimes with friends and sometimes with the family. The youthful nature in the true world will be an everlasting experience for everyone irrespective of age differences. The most experienced will have the equal wisdom in the perfect harmony and nobody will grow old, but only wisdom growth that won't cause any aging. When someone is drunk, they won't lose any sense or temper. The youthful nature will be so meaningful that we will never try to lose it and we will not lose it under any case or reason. This is the nature that caused us evil on earth and now it's been perfected in the true world for our happiness and glory. We cannot imagine a reality that could be less significant than the one felt on earth. The ever youth will fill in our every day and every moment lifestyle and that won't require any indecent acts. Everyone will be happy in their respective ways and we lost nothing in truth. The youthful nature in the true world is an everlasting perfection.

Chapter Ten:

Restaurants, Bars and Night Clubs

We will have specialty in every treat in the true world. The true world is everyone's imagination into a reality. Although there will be no hunger but wisdom growth, food will always be a choice in our appetite. We will enjoy food in style. There will always be something new in the taste and flavour. The nature will be a combined choice of all, and we will find it in every form in our pleasure. Since the energy we constitute is permanent and everlasting, our consumption in food will be cleared out in simple workout and the extra energy will pass out through burps and through cells in the skins. There will be no leftovers of any kind.

The restaurants in each country will contain the flavours of their choice. They will be dispensed in mechanics of processing nature by electronically controlled programmes that will fit in every restaurant. We will not require plants or animals for the ingredients. Each restaurant will be equipped with such mechanics of motion in processing nature into our common use and they will never run out of essentials. Whatever food we enjoyed here on earth; we will enjoy them again in unique style in perfection. The restaurants will operate round the clock but especially the evenings and the visitors will always be delightful combinations. Every performer will have a task of teaching and pleasing the visitors from all over the true world. It will function like a never-ending process and they will revisit in discovering the newness and flavour of one in many.

The architectural and colourful design of the restaurants will bear the significance of its existence and those suffered from hunger will never believe that hunger can be solved into a greater virtue of seeing and feeling its necessity, just a mere crime perfected to ever growth and timeless sustenance of life and its pleasure. Everyone will be happy, and all treats will be unique in its nature and origin. None will be overcrowded or understaffed nor even short of any qualities in taste or its quantity. The nature in fullest harmony for our enjoyment and excitement into an unlimited glory and that will last indefinite into the future.

Even each home will have the everyday essentials which will be delivered by the machines that processes nature and food in automation will deliver our choices, preparing the breakfast essentials if we ever hate a walk or journey to the common places. Every quality will always be on display at home or out of home. Hunger will find its common pursuit, the query in invention and intervention and the reason of global insecurity we face on earth. If someone starves, that will have no effect because, we will be complete in energy either in consumption or rejection and the food will only be a delightful combination, either one takes it or not, doesn't matter but it will measure the good intentions of ours and share the wisdom with all.

Beautifully designed bars will be a common place of gatherings of all couples and singles. Drinks will be served and dispensed from automatic units which will never run out. The favourite songs will fill the evenings and nights in absolute joy and glamour's. Everyone will share their experiences in life on earth and the happenings. The alcohol and wines will be in plenty. The drinks will never cause senselessness or addictions. The dispensing units will be connected to the bars from a common place of manufacture which will be processed from nature and they will be brilliant in taste and texture. The alcohol and wines will be superior in quality and taste and absolutely perfected.

The bars will contain indoor games for everyone's participation and that will display superior human quality, and none will hurt each other or lose patient of their qualities and behaviours. The alcohols and drinks will be carbon free. It may appear carbon free alcohol cannot exist but when the whole nature is perfected into the elements of light, the alcohols without carbon bonds will taste better than what we have found on earth. It will be the main function of hydrogen and oxygen into our biology giving far more superior feelings than any of the drinks that we tasted on earth. So, the carbonless drinks will not cause any leftovers will vaporise through our breaths and dispersing through body cells and will not require to visit washrooms or toilets.

One of the best attractions in the true world will be the night clubs where beauty will be a shared joy of all. The beautiful structure and their location will be the major tourist venue. The beauty of the lost will be in great harmony. The night clubs will invite all to those who had a say to such glory and pride. It will be filled in great joy and excitements. The beauty and its pain will glamourize the entire community. Especially those who died in this world becoming a casualty of war and crimes will be the best performers in display of their sacrifice and valuables. They all will enjoy in pairs which on earth was their perspective.

All the night clubs will bear its significance to the entire community. Those who never saw the peace and love in relationships will fill the night clubs in display of their great interest in love and harmony. Everyone will share their experiences in life and its pleasure in a manner that won't be any cause of concern of anyone. The glory will be an everlasting story in perfection and growth; of the most rewarded one's and their emotional resolutions brought into a reality. Each night will bear its allegiance in a most befitting manner and we all will share our experiences in life and the casual growth that affected us all.

Chapter Eleven:

Beauty Parlours

Beauty as a lesson is our most alike perspective in life. We all want to be liked by all. Everybody is not equally beautiful and attractive. But we enjoy beauty as a lesson. This lesson is one of the most important aspects of our life which brings an understanding in relationships. We all want to be loved by all and that's the main aspect in our images. Little bit of raise of such images carries a significant value in our thoughts and dreams. We all are created equal which we learn through life's lessons. Sometimes inner beauty is more important than outer one's and that's the possible reason of intelligence growth. We all are not equally beautiful and attractive but the understanding in such difference makes us unique in creation. We are the human's, the best in creation.

The true world is the creations of light and we all created from light will experience ever growth that is permanent and everlasting. Since we will be complete in energy and growth, we will not require any toilets or washrooms because the food that we consume will be one hundred percent digested and there will be no left overs or anything to discard from our biology except will convert them into burps or gases that body skin will discard and the growth also will be fixed one. But we enjoy beauty as our lessons.

Since growth will be fixed and our images remain a permanent identity, there will be some aspects which will allow us the necessity in improving our images. The growth in beauty can only be exercised in the growth of the nails and the hair; these two are the only ones that will help us in improving our images. We will be able to grow the nails and the hairs.

In the true world we will have beauty parlours that will help us in improving and designing our beautiful images by controlling the growth of our hair and nails and it will be on an instant basis. The image on hair colour or its growth can be fixed on an instant machine-controlled programming and such is the nails which we will design into the shape of our choice. We won't have to wait for days to measure for its growth and simple input in the machine is sufficient for its function towards our choice in specific design.

Since the nature won't cause us any effect on our body or our images, it will remain forever perfection. But we will again find the better beauty agents and perfumes with no side effects or leaving behind any wasteful products. Everyone will improve the quality in beauty by the makeup of their choice without any restrictions whatsoever and the beauty will be beautified colourfully in a most decent way to look beyond their imaginations and inspirations.

The cosmetics and the fragrances once used will again be recycled naturally and they will abound in with supplies. Even we will have image correcting laboratories which will correct any of the deformities even if it existed by any form or shape in an instant basis. The beauty will be so delicately nourished none will feel the absent of any senses in it. There will be no use of toilets or washrooms and nothing will cause any damage in us. We will be forever perfected into the elements of light. Beauty parlours will be the beauty makers and we will shine brighter than flowers.

Chapter Twelve:

Theatres and Concerts

The nearly twenty billion years in creation of fire and the whole universe will be projected by real happenings and the events surrounding this creation will occupy the theatres in real motion pictures. Every country and every city will have theatres, a major attraction of the true world. We will have real events displayed from the beginning of this creation in motion pictures. How the fire is lit? How we are created and what took place since then will always be a true story to find and discover. Every mystery concerning this creation is a recorded history. We will know what happened in this creation from its inception in a real show of power and evolution. The theatres in every country will have their specialty in presentation. All the fictions will represent the real truth behind a story. Nothing in human thought will remain unanswered. Even we will find the best thrillers and the comedians have a place in those recorded history of this creation. We will discover the intents of other powers in the creative pursuit and to learn and see if anyone had a better resolution to this creation or better perspective to another creation will be displayed in a historical perspective.

This entire creation and the creations beyond will be a reality to understand in logics and in motion. Every faculty in human thought will display in motion pictures. All the great humans and all the wars are a recorded event and we will know if ever a human missed anything in that faculty of thought. The science will be an absolute reality in understanding that we have achieved what we hoped for. Every body's estimation will be a real story in those theatres and if ever a human missed in a thought it will show us how we could be incompetent to one powerful writer that will say about our weaknesses and strengths in discovering if we humans ever missed anything in this creation or any creation so forth. In other words, nothing will remain unanswered either in human or any supernatural creation.

Every nation, every country and every city will have their respective theatres that will represent their ambitions and disciplines in a concrete manner including what happened or what will happen in a clear view of the past, present, and the future. Since the true world will be above our expectations, our intelligence will be enhanced by projecting anything we may have found incomplete or impossible in our thoughts to see and find if life ever had a question about our dreams, in other words, our thoughts and as good as our dreams are also in a controlled pursuit. We may seem it's a mystery; the true world may seem nothing a mystery.

The limitless parity in space and the science that fools us and limits our ability to explore will be well defined. And in the true world this limit will be overcome and anything that was impossible will be possible again. We will enjoy and learn the all events which don't require reoccurrence will be in motion pictures including love and harmony. The limits are set in moral standards and in the true world these standards will be respected by all. Since the death will be stopped, we will have superior intelligence on display and the motion pictures will represent such reality.

All the dramas will be a pleasant story to share. We will replica the kings and the queens. The rulings occurred in history will be a shared story and all our ambitions will display in a most meaningful way. We will recover all the lost senses and the great comedians will fill us in happiness and laughter's. Children will love the relationships and young will adore the beauty and none will be old enough than the time itself.

One of the most important revolutions will be the concerts that will unite all the cultures. It will be so diverse that everyone will understand each other. All the great artists of all times will be the reality in the true world. The music and the musical instruments will be so advanced that we will listen to it like a never-ending process. The songs will be unique, and the artists will be glamorous in both their appearance and performance. All the sad stories will be a true glory and will fill the airwaves in newness in tone and rhythm.

Every evening and night will signify its moments in true harmony. Since we don't have to work for a living, the tasks of all artists will invite the one who ever dreamt of becoming one. The joy and its fruits will be an everlasting experience and we all are here in the true world where we have nothing to do but enjoy each moment in the fullest terms in happiness and glory. The true world will let us explore life into an infinite reality.

Besides theatres and concerts, we also will have home entertainments in both movie and songs. We will explore the artists live when we have hopes to see them and how we socialise with them and learn in what takes to be a great performer or a leader. The qualitative analysis will make us unique in standard. All together we will have great joy and we will invent everything in its core value. We will invent everything in its newest form and reality that will beat any time on earth. The concerts will be the place to share our pain and its gain into the permanent future, the resounding True World.

Chapter Thirteen:

No mountains, Oceans, Lakes or Rivers

The True World will be absolutely in marble shape with no mountains, lakes or rivers. There will be no open grounds. The ground will be totally covered with emulsions by natural sources and chemical components. There won't be any kind of storms; rains, thunder or dust storms. Water will be holding in the center of the world without any kind of fire in existence. It will be a motion that will direct the water flow or flow of any type of natural products for human and the animal consumptions. The electronic control will fill all kinds of dispensing units for our use. The true world will be totally calibrated into grids and even molecular evidence will support its functions to the pinpoint in locating its specific place and its reference in our common use. Everything will be a recorded adventure, and we will discover the complete science in revolution. The perfect automation of matter, material and its relationship to life will bring newness in our thoughts and growth.

This world is a casual motion, that's why everything dismantles and disembarks. The geographical reason needs balance in motion and that's why the mountains are created to hold both the gravity and the motion. In the true world, the creation is a reality and there won't be any force detrimental to its gravity and motion, it will maintain the equilibrium of motion without causing any imbalance in either the gravity or motion. Therefore, there won't be any need of mountains or any higher objects to hold its stability. Because of the casual creation, the entire creation and the universe maintains the motion that needs a power waste and time frame existence, hence the creation of fire, where everything is casual which requires time in stability. In the true world time can be controlled as well as the motion for best reality and all creations of light are the realtors for such an ever-existing nature and the mechanics in complete automation.

In this world the motion of water breaks us apart. The oceans limit us in senses. A river or oceanic cruise lets us feel the limitless wisdom that is being in control. But it is true that we even have much higher ambition to enjoy the limitless when the space is opened its boundaries for our exploration and that limitless wisdom will let us feel that the necessity of water and its boundaries are overcome by more wider and intelligent choices. That's the discovery of the limitless creation, the True World where we will find hundreds of oceans in just a minute's adventure into the space filled in great joy and the discovery of such planets in existence.

When we talk about the rivers and the lakes or oceans the question of marine life comes into our mind. In the true world every city in every country will have huge aquariums where all the marine life will live in a pleasant display of science and creation. It will contain both types either salt or pure water creatures. Since everything is complete energy either in consumption or rejection, the marine life will be harmless to anyone or anything that is life or matter.

The communication and transportation will be absolutely perfected. The entire true world will be connected to all by both land and air. We will travel to distant places and will learn limitless parity that bonds us like a statesman or a fellow citizen. We will enjoy the arts and culture of many nations around the true world. The communication will be simple and easy, readily available to all. The borders and the boundaries of each country will bear its ensemble in unique display of murals and high banners. The foods will delight us as a new flavour never found it before. The food will be dispensed from machines processing nature for any ingredients of our choice including the taste of marine life. Therefore, there will be no need for depending on any type of livestock.

Since the countries will be divided by boundaries without any waterways, we will feel it an easy access to any part of the true world. For travel by air, we won't require any runways for airplanes for takeoff, because the aircrafts are gravity controlled and the simple input into the computer will both takeoff and land in exact location and specification without even the requirements of float devices. From takeoff to landing it will be an absolute control in sustenance both in the air and on the ground, there won't be any crushing force. The True World will have all the qualities of water and fluids that rests underground processed by mechanics and dispensed on demand.

Chapter Fourteen:

Live Zoo's and Prehistoric Animals

This creation is simply fascination since everything evolves. It will evolve till we all found the end of such evolution and after this creation if anything is possible is nothing but the reality that we all existed and will exist into infinity. This infinite growth is now a question how is it possible to go back in time? The perfect control is such that we don't have to go back but go into the future which will recognize and replenish all true creation. Why do we have to say the true creation? That's the common question to answer. Yes, an intelligent creation is not indefinite but everlasting and that's the power of truth.

In the true world we will have all the creations that went through the passage of time. Because there is no theory intelligent enough than what the nature confronted us. It's definitely true that they all are existing and will be existing beyond any question. All those animals that existed on this earth will live in the true world and they will be relocated in the common place for each stage in creation. We all see and enjoy the creativity in live sensation. They will live in different part of the true world according to their time frame in existence on earth.

A tiger or a lion will not be found where the dinosaurs live. There will be parks that will designate the time of their existence. All animals and the creatures will live in their respective places and we will watch what was a memory is now a reality. They also will be complete in energy and the creations of light so, obviously all animosities will be discarded. But they also will display superior creation by sharing with us the sense and the pursuit in our adventure. We will follow by certain tracks in their dwelling places and they will act and admire our presence. This live Zoo's will be away from any human habitation and we will visit them whenever we feel. They all will be divided both by scientific and historical perspectives.

On the other hand, the domestic animals especially, the pets will live with us including the horses but not the farm animals as they will also have a separate place for their own independence and enjoyment which they earned by sacrifice. A true creation can be both human and an animal; both will exist in the true world. It will be a great joy for all true creations. All animosities will have no use, since all will be happy, and we won't require an animal for any of our use. The animal kingdom will be far more superior in design and they will display on our civility an outstanding achievement in life and we will feel sorry for misuse.

In this world certain animals are including the smaller ones like the mosquitoes, 'bugs and any harmful pests will not exist beyond this creation, because they are also created from fire and when fire is resolved their existence also will be stopped. The true world will be a true endeavour in design, and we will not lose any of the creations of light. The animals of the creations of light will always be on display in their respective places. We also will have the record of the events that took place on this earth and reasons of their extinctions. They will be always happy in the true world and we will enjoy creativity in live display without causing any harm to them or by them.

Chapter Fifteen:

The English Wisdom

In the True World the English Wisdom will be the greatest victory of all in unique discipline and virtue in both by moral and scientific adventures. The best attraction of this or any creation for any time will be the English Wisdom. All the dreams of humans and the great merchants will be the reality in the English wisdom. The English Wisdom will be the English continent the greatest and most famous in its origin and creation of the true world. This is where all the English-speaking people will live, and it will be the biggest and most splendorous continent of the true world where all the vibrant civilisations will rest and function. The True Worlds major functions will be projected and controlled from the English continent. The English continent will be most diverse in arts and culture.

End of evolution is the victory of a family and any empirical formula will attain that reality. We all will be represented by family and friends. When the evolution ends It will be the resounding glory initiated right from our earth into the infinite wisdom of the true world. The true world will then start functioning in full scale when one family becomes the power and authority of all the events that took place on earth and its projection into the future, the true worlds existence becomes a perfected reality of anything created from light. We will live and enjoy in the true world as long as we wanted. The English Wisdom will remain the best continent unmatched by anything in creation for any time. Also, it will remain the best attraction in knowledge, invention and wisdom. Everyone around the world will have a hope to visit the English Wisdom. It represents the superior quality and performance of matter, material and mechanics both in motion and growth. Although growth will be stabilized but we will exercise habitual growth that won't cause us aging.

All the memory and controllability will be stored in the English Wisdom from where it will be directed according to calendar and time. We all will know each moment's reality and truth. Nothing will remain unknown to anyone and nothing will happen from its own. It will be absolute factor of events that take place around the true world and the universe or the entire creation as a whole perspective. All will be informed and we all will know what to expect now and, in the future, it will be accurately predicted and no mishaps. The English Wisdom will be superior in design, nature and architect. The cities and towns will be filled by great joy and excitements. The amusement parks and live concerts will inspire us all to share some moments in truth. The English Wisdom will remain open to all the inhabitants of the true world and everyone will have a hope to feel the glory by sharing their knowledge and experience.

We all dream, and that dream is a reality in the true world. The English Wisdom will dominate in that dream. It is hope of all mankind that our expectations are fulfilled in the pursuit of creation and a memory must not be lost. The English wisdom will uphold our values and we will be together again in the perfect discipline of the true world. The scientific evidences of such existence will be in a clear proof that life can begin again in full harmony without leaving any absences from our hearts and minds. This common glory of mankind will be rejuvenated with new and more accurate creation, an everlasting perfection; the true world. The English Wisdom will honour any composers with dignity and respect towards the fruitful end of the current creation, the end of evolution and the end of the creations of fire.

The English wisdom will be the center of focus of all true creations that existed on this earth. We all will follow through the cycle in creation and reach a place, called The True World and the English Wisdom upholds our values in assurance of such a reality that; it can exist and it will definitely exist and a true memory will never be lost. The English Wisdom will be the most beautiful continent of all or any creation and will be represented by a family, the core value in our dream. It will inspire us into highest ambition that a truth never fails, and the English Wisdom will uphold all our expectations into a perfect reality.

When the evolution comes to an end, our family in wisdom will guide and direct us towards the safe passage of time and growth in perfect and accurate control, a mind in true motion that can redirect the motions of danger and destruction to a halt and discard when needed. We will find the safe passage to infinity and the controllability will rest in us, in other words a superior machine in design in our full control and we will redirect and diminish the motions that are harmful or unsafe. A strongest mind in action, the strongest family in wisdom, the core value of the English Wisdom. A singular momentum in a mind in superior design will unfold the controllability factors in creation that can process and divert the motions of casual creation; the creations of fire will cease, and the creations of light will dominate.

The English Wisdom will remain in full control of the true world as well as the fruitful end of the creations of fire. In the true world there will be nothing happening from its own, it will be an absolute control and we all will know the certainty in creation and its nature of evolution, there will be nothing of concern or worries. The English Wisdom will dominate the true world in every respect, say it science, culture or arts. English will be the international language of the true world and will be understood by all. Even those who never knew a single alphabet in English will be fluent in just few lessons. English as a language and culture will dominate the true world in every respect and they will also know and use their own languages widely within their communities. English as a whole will dominate the true world in every respect.

The English Wisdom will unite us altogether irrespective of differences. All the happenings and the future perspective will be a recorded motion picture which will educate us what to expect in the future. Nothing will remain unknown or nothing will happen from its own. The recorded projection of the past will unfold all the events that took place on this earth since its beginning as the creations of fire. We will know everything from the past and towards the future in clear messages. The English wisdom will open up our ambition into a new perspective by allowing us to invent and conquer the mystery in creation that is still unknown to us. Everybody will hope to reach their expectations and the English Wisdom will let them discover what was impossible before. All the information's of all times will be available in the English Wisdom's recorded memories; therefore, we will be able to predict the future and our interest most accurately. Most importantly time will be in our control, so, we lose nothing. The English Wisdom is our absolute perfection and we will control the infinite existence.

All the true world's major events will be controlled and projected by the English Continent. It will be so beautiful and eventful of surprises that the English continent will be recognized as the best continent. Every moment of truth will grow in perfect harmony and we have only one purpose in living; enjoy life to its fullest bloom. Everyone in the true world will have a hope to visit the English continent and they will express their gratitude in a most honourable way and enlighten the glory in creation.

Everything in creation is a recorded will in which the motion trespasses through the events. We the living creation feel it as a happening truth. When we will discover the controllability factors, the entire creation will open up its pursuit and we will be sure that nothing happens from its own. The future thus will be an informative adventure of all, and we will enjoy life to its rightful cause. Our existence will become truth and we will live into the infinite reality that cannot be destroyed by any power. The everlasting glory will solve any issues that required the proof of power. Wisdom is the absolute power if ever a power needs to defend, that will be the English Wisdom in its complete reality. The glory in creation will be upheld by the English continent through perfect control and ruling, and if ever a creative power in ambition or higher motivation, we will face it through better prospect. If that power is weaker in strength, we will win it and if that power is more logical and accurate of the future prospect, there will be no shame in accepting the defeat and the truth cannot be harmed under any circumstances. We will live and we will shine into the infinite growth; finally, our existence is the truth.

Chapter Sixteen:

Perfect Control and Ruling

In the True World everyone will understand their civic rights. Even the nature will be in good harmony with us and there will be no causes of any type of danger. Since death will be stopped, there will no reason to try or break a law or a momentum of infinite growth and sustenance. Each country and each nation will understand the superior design in creation that will share great joy, and death and destruction will be an impossible fact. There will be no reason of animosity, since we won't find any of the causes or reasons of such habits. All our necessities and needs will be met to the specific of the demand, and there will be none of the events that lead to power struggle since everyone will be happy in whatever form or shape, they are in.

Each country and each nation will be represented by leadership. They will direct and guide inter-state visits. We all will enjoy the resources of the true world in a planned way so that all doesn't end up in one place of interest. It will be directed according to the input of information's stored and generated in a timely manner. Nobody will miss out any of the attractions of the true world and it will be a composite in nature. The best interest will be the beauty contest held in each state with the stories binding in their life experiences and the abuses surrounding their living hood. It will be beautifully projected throughout the true world ceremonies. Each nation will invite the other to share the moments of joy and truth.

The most intelligent will always be honoured and respected in every form and every fact of life. None will lose patience of their qualities and it will always display its nature by every sphere of life and its common goal. The entire creation will be calibrated scientifically and by nature and we will find the right perspective in living and loving. Our superior intelligence will include everyone in the family and friends, even children will be the great performers. The competitions in intelligence will let us share our thoughts in a most beautifully and realistically propagated way what happened in life on earth and what they have learned. The beautiful and sad stories will always inspire us into an infinite growth shared by all. The most intelligent will always rule the lesser intelligent but it will make no difference in individual understanding and compromise. The entire world will be fabricated in perfect growth and harmony leaving nobody unaccounted for in any circumstances.

There will be no cause for abuse, violation or a crime. Everybody will be happy, and nothing will be left short from our hearts and minds. We will enjoy superior growth and discipline that is respected by all. If there is a concern it will be dealt with instantly and since death will be stopped none will face any of the causes of death. Even if someone tried a jump from a hundred story building, the rate of fall will be controlled by the true world gravity, the impact on the ground will be as smooth as a mere touch down without sustaining any bodily injury or harm.

The current vacuum of space is only the reasons of creations of fire and when fire is relieved from its task, light will take over its functions and the reasons in vacuum and the pressure will be nominal throughout the universe. We will not require temperature control or pressurization to reach any distance; even we will breathe whenever it's a necessity. The creations of light can sustain beyond any limits that we face in the creations of fire. The perfect control in the true world will be both scientifically and in human nature a realistic dream. None will find any of the causes of death or injury, not even aging.

The scientific and moral gain will surpass any of the causes of lawlessness or crime. But we will have wished to feel the limitless and that will be the future in our invention and motive. Beside that we will always find something new every day. The glory in the true world will fill everyone's imagination into a reality. The true world will evolve with a similar calendar of ours into a timeless peril. We will not have to work for a living or support anyone in need but it will be filled with so much of inspirations that we will never try to miss it by any circumstances and it will be an everlasting glory and our work will be to enjoy and share the infinite wisdom with all.

Philosophy may never soothe us until the scientific evidence of control are proven to be effective. It definitely is the pursuit of the most intelligent, who knows everything in creation and has the control over any thoughts and perceptions and can prove that it is possible and of course by a human of vast knowledge and intelligence. A rapid transition of motion towards that fruitful end is everyone's hope that we will control infinity as per our choice and a perfect control is just a mere happening truth. We will live beyond death, because we are the most intelligent species. Recovery is our goal to sustain into infinity, lost by time and death, no problem; we will also control time and redesign the future filling in with all true creations that existed since the time began to evolve with nature.

Chapter Seventeen:

Kiosks and Shopping Malls

Anyone for drive by treats? No problems! The kiosks and the shopping malls will be a major point of our momentary happiness. We will know what to expect. Every corner of the streets will be recognized by a presence of kiosks that will operate both by us and in automation. It will have dispensing units for short treats including ice creams, pops or candy and you won't require any coins to get it, neither will it run out of supplies. It will process nature and produce you your demand with no exceptions. Highly motivated to drive, yes, the staffed one's will share your smile and will promote your ambition to come back again. Kiosks are a specialty for a shorter treat or an intention to experience what we have missed on earth. Got an empty cup and aren't sure what to do with it, go no further, put it in the automatic recycle machine it will dispense you the same one upon hundred percent recycle, if don't need it right away, don't ask for it. Broken glass no problems just hold the extended chord of the recycler, hundred percent absorbed and instantly recycled. More fascinating is that nothing is a waste or a concern. That's why children will always break glasses and plates because they want more.

Although our homes will be fully furnished with everything included including the recycling machines, but we will always think for design and comfort. The design is replaceable only the things that are easily decorate able, like the clothes, curtains or bed sheets. The heavier stuffs are permanent will never be destroyed and minor repairs are just a fuss. The shopping malls will contain all our needs if there is any. Want a pair of shoes or a dress? That's where mostly we will use the shopping malls. In other words, display of fashion and wander together. Your shoe will never be destroyed neither your dresses but if you change it, can be replaced without any cost or concern. Everything is hundred percent recyclable and will not cause any ecological affect.

While the beauty and fashion will always be on display, our intentions to win all will be the difference and surprise of many, seeking friendship and love for ever. The clothes will also be delivered with a simple input into the machine that will require all your specifications including size and shape, it will dispense with no mistake. Although our homes and the dwelling units will have the machines that will dispense various types of foods and drinks but there will be exceptions where the shopping malls carrying different menu items for our consumptions, we will always measure the taste and quality of such products in abundance, if we want to prepare something different than usual, there will be plenty available and ready to use.

The complete nature and the combination of mechanics in motion will deliver any of the taste or thrill if ever one missed in his life and nothing will be impossible except the creation of fire. Every quality of light and its product will be far more superior to what we felt and tasted on earth throughout its creation. And every quality of matter, material and the nature in it will display whatever choice we had in seeing it into a reality will be the perfect growth and will satisfy our needs and pleasures indefinitely.

Chapter Eighteen:

The Intelligence, Games and Sports

In the true world every homes and dwelling units will be fitted with audio and video entertainment systems including live broadcasts in and around the world. We will know every moment's events and they will inform us the current and the future events that take place round the clocks. Our intelligence will be displayed in a unique manner and we all will know what to expect in any time of our choice and we will plan ourselves accordingly. We will have superb intelligence on display. Nothing will happen from its own and it will be a perfect control around the world. One family will occupy in wisdom and that family will have the access and control all over the true world and the stored information of any happenings and growth. They will be joined by the family of nations around the world. Even the inter-state and continental visits will be monitored by careful planning. The space missions and the adventures into the unknown galaxies and universes will be open to all mankind. We will enjoy and discover the limitless invention in creation in a very simple and effective manner. We will know whatever took place in the past and will take place in the future in a most meaningful way and nothing will be a mystery or unknown. We all will be adequately informed and there will be no concerns of anything that will hurt our feelings.

All the mysteries in creation will open up its significance in a clear and concise manner; none will have any questions or worries. We will seek and measure intelligence if any power or authority is more informed than us and if they have better perspective than us. We will invade other creations if there is any beyond the limits of our existence. We will seek the better solution than of ours and everyone will have a task to fulfill their ambitions in discovering the limitless growth and parity. The entire creation will be a clear and well-informed source of our existence and it will maintain its principle in an effective control and ruling. Since we will have indefinite growth and sustenance, we will control our dreams towards a meaningful end if ever we wished to see what could be a repetition in creation and creating back the fire and the creations of fire, not until anyone disputes including a child or anyone who opposes it by any means or reasons.

The unique and most authentic sources of information's will readily be available for anyone seeking it. It will be absolutely accurate. In the true world nothing will be a worry or concern and we will live there as long as we want. We will watch if any power is more informed than us and it will never be possible because our inventions are more logical and infinite in nature by creating back the light in its dominant role, the origin and source of all creations. Anything that represents superior creation must master the light and its control. This light and its motion are our intelligence, vision and pursuit. To create and control infinity or any creation that needs light will be nothing but our own dream and existence. We share our intelligence in many ways, most notably the games and sports. It qualifies us as a most fit person both in intelligence and strength. If we only have intelligence but not strength, we are virtually a handicap. On the other hand strength gives us hope that we can defend ourselves in the event of a catastrophe or disaster and we can rebuild ourselves from the lost values.

In the true world this activity will be far more superior since we will know everything from the past, the present and the future. Our intelligence will be far more superior and we will compete in games and sports in a most friendlier way not letting anyone down or anyone feeling neglected and since there will be no sorrow or pain of any kind, the other will find its rightful place in a game and sports. In the true world we will have all kinds of entertainment and that will not harm or cause any defect on anyone for others superiority. The intelligence will be most wisely displayed all the time, and none will fit in all games and one may not fit in all games either. There will be games and sports that will promote friendship and trust.

If we knew what the outcome in a game could be or In a sport, we would need better kind of event that will display our hobbies and ambitions. Since the true world will be a complete perfection nothing will be mystery or unknown. We will play and enjoy the sports that raise our intelligence and establish bond between ourselves. All the players who played professionally and the amateur players will understand that we even have a greater glory than to compete and win the weaker ones. All the games and sports in the true world will be most harmonious and peaceful. The fittest person is none but everyone irrespective of their age and gender.

We will discover new sports and that will require new skills and tactics. It may involve physical or mental strength to qualify but it will never let one's concern that any of the games can defeat the other disrespectfully or if anyone has any concern. In this world we have games that are tied up culturally and geographically. In the true world these games will be more diverse and with more new ways to compete. The idea is all intelligence will be unique by nature and that won't harm anyone's qualities. The games and sports are also a place of gathering and the intelligence in the true world will be so diverse that even a child player will fill the joy and happiness.

The true world will maintain its superiority by all counts and since we don't have to work for a living, the beautiful bands, the parade and dance of stars will be ever memorable incidents. Those who were in the forces, the beautiful rhythm of their boots on March coupled by the music will be an addition in everyday routine in showing off the perfect discipline that we are in. Everybody will be a celebrity in their own fields of choice and interest, and we will discover the true world, an everlasting glory in the history of creation.

Chapter Nineteen:

Recreation of Fire and This Earth

Entire creation is a revival perception. In the true world we all will have a hope to renew our dreams. We will understand that a truth can never be destroyed neither any power can sustain without a sacrifice. And this sacrifice of ours will be understood by all and we will have comfort in thinking that we will wish to experience the casual motions back again by recreating fire and its creation back into reality. We will always understand that we always existed here in the true world by then it will be time immemorial and will have an interest for a passage through the creations of fire. This fire is also created from light and it is the casual motion of light. Hence this earth and the whole universe is ultimately the casual motion and it is the main reason that we suffer death and destruction.

When the fire is created the absolute vacuum also created by its affect. It is the reason of our confinement into a limit and anything beyond earth remained a mystery. Creating back fire is the cycle in creation and we all lost memory once and we are now in the transit of recovering our memories back again since the current creations of fire is coming to an end. The light is the universal source in creation, and it will maintain its superiority by all account in life and the matters. When we go back to the true world, we will realize that we always existed here, and our memories will be complete.

In the true world we understand that we go to the creations of fire for a lesson of few years. Although the age and time of fire may be twenty billion years evolution, we will not face sudden impact of losing everything. The time that we feel now is comfortable to dream back to reality. All the creations of light and matter will pass through this evolution until we gain the intelligence of recovering ourselves from the creations of fire.

The true world will hold our values in every way, and nobody will fear the creations of fire. It will maintain a safe passage for humans, plants and animals. When the fire is engaged, the creations of fire then will start the process in evolution. They all will leave the true world without any shock or pain. When the creations of fire are ready for sustenance of life and nature, those prehistoric animals will be the first occupants and will relocate themselves into that world. When time comes for the humans, we will be resolved and dispersed like memory dispersal.

Besides the creations of light, there are many creations that are created absolutely from fire and they are the sole creations of fire and they only come into existence when the fire is created. They will be both in humans and animals. Most importantly the humans that are created solely from fire are represented by the carbon bond. We will be able to differentiate them by their nature and acts.

This carbon will maintain its growth until its time comes to an end like today's nature and reality.

We will know everything in the true world including time of the recreation of fire. Since we are already in this world, we are now into the transition of losing the creations of fire or we can say goodbye to the creations of fire. We will be sorry to lose all the creations of fire since it can't exist beyond its time frame. Those created from fire will have a hope to see their dream come true only into the next terms of events when the fire is recreated. We now know from this world that what were the causes of incompetency to sustain into the infinity. We are greatly divided by our thoughts and actions. This is the reason of abuse and casualties. Our sufferings are also related into that aspect of creation.

The true world will be an astounding success story in the history of creation, and we will never fear our passage through this world. Even the animals also maintain their choice of living into the permanent glory, the creation of light. When we reach the true world, we will understand that we always existed here, and everything will be a complete sense. Nobody will be sent to this world or the creations of fire won't start until the tiniest living creature to the smartest one disputes their intention to face creations of fire again. We understand that this world is not a place of total harmony for anyone and nobody have intentions to face it again, that's very true. This world won't be created until and unless everyone agrees with it, because truth as a power has control over anything from happening and that is our intelligence best understood by all.

Although the creations of fire don't have reality to understand or even knowledge to realize, they will always be interested to live in this world for ever, one of the dirtiest and most casual natures one could ever imagine is this world and the creations of fire. The creations of fire don't have any answer if ever they cease to exist or face death, they have no perception and only would imagine even a wilder dream upon death but no perception of what it could be as a real creation. Because, their memories are wrong and mostly casual in nature. Also, will believe in higher power and an impossible reality.

The creations of fire is not limited between this world and the humans, the whole universe is on a standard setting and that's why it's difficult to explore because of casual motions. In the true world all the causes of casual motion will be understood, and it won't limit us in either invention or sustenance into the infinity. We will come to this world only when we wish and there is none to force us into impossible dreams. This is our choice of why this world will be recreated.

Chapter Twenty:

Love, Respect and Humanity

This world is the combination of our choices. Either we die in peace or raise a concern to escape a death. But it's true that we will control the future into a definite reality and that is represented by our thoughts and actions. Nobody likes to be dishonoured or disrespected but when there is a trouble, it is difficult to escape either. Because we still have hopes. The true world exists in everyone's dreams and prayers. The time may answer our concerns rightfully. The control of this reality rests with the person proven to the most intelligent creation and we will find out what are the cause and effect of the time and growth. To stop that cause will require an accurate flow of information's that are rightfully explained, and the complete reality is well understood. If one knows we all know and how to prevent a happening is what is unsafe or to regulate what is a safe passage into the infinity. We all will follow that information which is most accurate and true.

Love is the most important aspect in human endeavour, and this is the only reason we are the best of creation. We must love every human in equal harmony irrespective of race, colour, sex, religion. This is the bond between family and friends. When we reach the true world, we will have complete wisdom in control and ruling, which mean we will be into a perfected growth that will last into infinity. Since there will be no limit of wealth, we will have only one reality; enjoy life to its fullest. Every life will find its rightful place, and none will be unhappy by any reasons. In this world love is understood casually and we will deplore the causes that make us different from one another. Entire creation will be glorious in its every essence and pursuit. There will be occasions to share the greater harmony which was impossible in this earth before. Each moment in each day will be filled in complete glory. We will share everyone's story about life in both arts and culture. The uniqueness of such display of our ambitions will fill in every part of the true world. Every child will be the greatest performers and will show off their merit in a most pleasant and delightful way, everyone will love them. Here on earth those children who never saw glory will be in ornamental display of their talent and virtue. They will be so appreciative of the true world that we will understand their pain in a most meaningful and smartest way. The children in the true world will be the symbol in glory and they will be the most major attractions of the true world.

The elderly and the sick people here on earth are the subject of our negligence because we couldn't find their importance in our life. Nobody needs a lesson in pain, but it is given anyway. Literally, a handicap is as much neglected as the subject itself. A little bit of respect to their pain is enough for that person to hope the future. They are the abuses of the nature. The best hope is also designed after them because they are so perfected that they won't harm another life for its own pleasure. They are the innocent sufferers of our heavens. Although they observe in silence but felt compassionate to the life in full harmony and wishes the same growth among them and all. Our simple respect to their causes makes us great and still such causes are unknown in existence, why it should be in that way. But it's true that we all are not created equal, but we learn equality in lessons and this lesson is one of the important aspects of our dream. The negative side of disrespect could be as bad as becoming a mystery. Of course, mystery is for those who are the reasons of immaterialism in creation, can't exist towards a fruitful end. Every life is meaningful when one is the most respected individual and gives a way for others to shine. The sad story is that there is a dream that can't exist beyond this creation and more notably the life and matters of creations of fire. Their all ambitions will be overcome in this earth and they are materially impossible to exist into the creations of light. That doesn't mean they lose respect of ours, in fact we will hold them glory whenever they ask for it into the recreation of fire. Love makes us unique and respect make us angelic.

In this world we are constrained by resources and that's the probable reason we work hard for our survival. There are more poor people than the riches. The fair share of our commonwealth is laid out in law and order. No one can find a resolution unless agreed by the conditions of a civil order in a society or a nation. But still people will be looking for shortcuts and that's in our human nature. On the other hand, many people don't care about the future, resulting in calamities and starvations. It may not be possible to educate the whole world, but we do our part, taking care of the humanity in trouble. And humanity is meant to cause trouble; otherwise this world will not be of any significance to us. This is the intelligence display of Master of Science and ethics; the moral is a common ground in understanding in that ethics. We help where we can reach.

Love, respect and humanity are our common destiny in education which binds us as a social being. From this world we discover the limits in hope and find the reasons of casual growth. The true world will be the ultimate discovery of ours in sharing the glory with all. The most intelligent creation may ask this creation, when does the pursuit to such discovery end and our quest for knowledge goes on towards that reality. It's true that one person cannot give the resolutions to these questions all by himself but when we are an educated will, we will find the reasons of our existence and the infinite growth is just a mere cause,

The true world will definitely dominate the intelligent creation. It will no longer be a doubt or perception. We will be able to find the motions of this earth in a revised flow of information's that will show us the safe way to embrace the events that caused us death and the death will be won. The creations of light then will occupy its predominant place in creation, the everlasting existence.

Chapter Twenty-One:

The Proof of Power

The proof of power comes into question when we have difference in thinking. One thought is right and the other is wrong. The wrong often recognizes the lesser power and keeps challenging the true power. This is the reason of mistrust and misrepresentation giving rise to conflict and chaos. The true power emerges from all the situations into a perfected strength and can sustain in any challenge or any situation, recognized by its unique discipline in growth and harmony. The lesser power revolves until the true power attains its momentum into an infinite growth. The casualties throughout this creation both by men and nature warn us about the possible outcome caused by the intentions of the lesser power. On the other hand, the true power maintains its superiority in both the belief and the reasons. When we understand the reasons of such casualties, we assume perfection in its play, the main philosophy of the true power. Whereas, the lesser power maintains its agony and the primary cause of mass extinction takes its effect on humanity. The difficult trends lets us believe that the true power controls everything including the lesser power, only to raise awareness among us that the best moral strength is recognized as the only glory of mankind that can last into infinity and a challenge by lesser power ensures us that it's a reasonable creation in trust. The lesser power is nothing more than a trouble.

The proof of power can be in two ways, either by might or in logics. It is laid out throughout the history in creation of such proofs and logics. Our intelligence is the main tool to understand the presence of a power. We all will have questions rather than answers, because, our existence is in doubt instead of a reality. We need proof that we can exist into infinity and in that aspect, we design dreams hoping that we all someday come together to live for ever or any reality that can answer our worries and concerns. The proof of power can assure us that there is some one that cares our welfare and promise us infinite future and a true memory can never be lost irrespective of the death and destruction that differs us from one another. We need proof of power that can defend our rights and can show us the path to infinite wisdom, and we don't want to die or why our existence should become a mystery. The proof of power is everyone's common choice as to why there are casualties in life and how can we recover our lost ones. The proof of a power is in the form of casualties, and the causes are our sensation to understand him who ruins everything in our lives and that power is in its essence of gaining the momentum. When we all have the same question, the power also is as simple as an answer that he is with us to renew our dream and the motion to infinite growth is a controlled pursuit, it's only a matter of time that the truth will unfold the presence of that power among us.

The proof of power comes in effect when comparing between two powers. If the two powers are equal in strength, none can win. One has to be more powerful than the other in order to win. Because when two powers in fight, since both has the same strength it will result in a draw. Suppose two snakes of same strength takes up a fight, both will end up in a draw, because none can win the other over strength. It was also laid out in historical perspective long ago when the human intelligence was in incipient stage. When the prophet Moses was challenged by the Pharaoh's magician, it was proved right. Moses was challenged by the Pharaoh's magician in the proof of strength. The magician challenged Moses by throwing out a snake which was hurling towards Moses and Moses then threw his stick which became even a bigger snake and ate the magicians snake. Although Pharaoh being not accepted the defeat Moses knew that an evil can never be perfected rather than destroyed by its own nature which was indeed result of such lesser power that Pharaoh's were destroyed.

This incident in history proves that when competing between two powers one must be more powerful than the other in order to win and this creation is never a reality of two competing powers. If we compare in science, nobody can hit two pins of equal sizes head on; even it's not possible by any machine to hit two pins head on, since the two pins point of contact will be impassable between one another. It's only possible by a power that controls magnetism, to hit the two pins head on. If the two hits head on in any way it still will be two objects that can assimilate but will not be possible between two powers in conflict of equal strength. What we learned from the Moses challenge that one power must be the greater than the other to win. If we could control magnetism one object has to be bigger than the other so that the bigger one absorbs the smaller one into its own strength. That's how the proof of power is laid down. If ever two powers in creation comes into question, it will be measured of who has the superior quality in force that can divert or destroy the casual motions that destroy us. If it ever found our infinite reality is just a moment's task.

The proof of power then came down into three major ideological beliefs. Notably Judaism, Christianity and Islam. In Judaism the proof of power came down in strength and logics, In Christianity the proof of power came down in creativity and in Islam, it came down in prayers. Although all the religions are ultimately the prayers that define power but its only Christianity where the creative hope was nourished by the unique role in creation, the Sacrifice. Because this entire creation is nothing but sacrifice of a true power, who has hopes for all. This power is still a total mystery to discover until that power faces his own creation and relieves us from the touch of evil and destruction.

The proof of power does not differentiate us from one another, but it definitely raises our intelligence to a superior creation. The presence of power among us also will follow through the events that take place around us which in turn nothing but our own will in perfection. In this modern age we will not be fooled of anything supernatural rather than the complete control of the events that take place around us. And then the events will be correctly predicted towards our common safety from the forces of destruction. Since this entire creation is based on two realities, the creations of fire and the creations of light, the creations of light will indeed pass through the transitions towards a perfected growth into an infinite wisdom.

The creations of fire as it faces its own reality will have the questions that required the correct nature of its ambiguity will never calm down until a force gives them a final resolution. They will always fail in vision and their perception into the future will be an impossible reality and they will rely on a lesser power, the power of confusion and mistrust. The essence of a true power creates the lesser power for its own growth, that's why a lesser power is also a necessity in creation of its existence, and all the acts of nature counts its glory in creation which is felt and which will be a permanent for the creations of light into the next creation. There is one power that will control all the powers, the creations of light.

Here in this world we face the proof of power by casualties and the causes are our lessons to learn about what to expect if the power would face us creation. Of course, hope is the common goal for all to see and find what we have missed in the pursuit of creation. The creation of good ambition is everyone's dream and we embrace them in our everyday life and the happenings are the clear signals of the essential growth. The only way to greater creation is the power of truth, the truth that holds every moment as a useful growth into the future. The proof of power will be as simple as an ambition which we design through knowledge and intelligence. This intelligence of ours is the primary criterion of this creation. It will ensure us that the growth can be stabilized, and the death can be stopped.

The question of power will always dominate in our thought until the evil is destroyed. This evil is the sole purpose of the lesser power to cause peace and create disharmony among all. When evil is given with the destiny and understood by all, the true power will turn into an everlasting glory. Since the true power ascends through evil and the lesser power, the lesser power has a necessity in our dreams. As soon as the true power gains its momentum, the lesser power will start to cease from existence and become a memory in creation.

When we all are perfected enough, we will dominate as the creations of light and the use and the question of power will become a meaningless motion, since evil finds its own destiny to belong, a total loss of intelligence will then surprise us creation and there will be none to defeat but everyone is a winner. The true power, an everlasting truth, defended by its own virtue and a task in imperil; death is won. We will turn into an immortal being. To redirect the motions that caused us death, it will be as easy as simply wishing it by all true creations, the creations of light into a permanent glory.

Creativity is the main theme in creation found in Christian theology and the logical proof of a power which was revealed more than two thousand years ago by God through Jesus Christ. We are now in the edge of that time for recurrence of the events that took away Jesus Christ's life from us. His reappearance will merely be a proof that he existed and will exist again into the infinite creation. It's only matter of time when he returns back on earth and take all true creations into the world of perfection where we will be joined together with our family and friends. The smooth transition will merely be a proof that a light can never be destroyed, and it can form anything into a reality in existence.

The true world is an absolute perfection which exists in our memory and in truth. The limitless wisdom can be controlled for our joy and pleasure and we will understand the reasons in creation and its follow up through generations. The time for such fruitful growth is now and we are on the edge of that reality. We will denounce power and we will be undefeatable by any reason or virtue. The exact nature and its occurrences lie in everyone's thought and imagination. Nobody's estimation will be left untouched and the true world will be our complete dream in succession which will beat any time on earth or any glory that is the creations of fire. The question of power will then turn into a memory in us and we will replace that with higher ambition and enjoy creativity in what was impossible before on earth. The true creation in the true world is a perfect harmony of nature and science that will last into infinity. All the logics in the necessity of power will clearly be understood by all and we will say them goodbye unto the next creation. The light will remain our complete wisdom in creation that can create and recreate anything of our choice. That's our victory in creation for ever and it will never end. We just lost memory for once through the creations of fire and now is the time to regain our confidence in creation and design our dream most intelligibly and we don't need power but hope. It's true that we existed and will exist into the future and we don't need power to prove that but only our wisdom.

The proof of power is the logical sequence in any creation which gives rise to the question in existence. Since we encounter casualties by motion, our expectations are similarly beyond the motions that caused us damage. We will be undefeatable by any power or might. The proof of power will be as simple as our hopes; that a dream cannot be defeated by any power or might. Our ambitions, motivations and expectations are more logical than any power that can dream of. The proof of power will be as simple as a wish. And we inherited it right; instead of power, we found in merit. And instead of might, we found in a beautiful dream. The True World an everlasting perfection.

Made in the USA
Columbia, SC
24 July 2020

14640843R00064